Run!

J.J. Smiley

Published by J.J. Smiley, 2022.

RUN!

First edition. December 25, 2022.

Copyright © 2022 J.J. Smiley.

ISBN: 979-8215605707

Written by J.J. Smiley.

Table of Contents

For my grandchildren.

Escape

AFTER CONCEALING THE nuclear weapon under some rocks, Rob pulled the pins from the plasma grenades and tossed them back over his head. Forty feet away, the formidable multi-sectional soldier bugs that had crawled into the next blast hole blew into a thousand little pieces. With a short reprieve, he and Matt jumped down into the ravine, hoping to put a little distance between them and their pursuers. We need to get as far away as possible; this nuke should take this whole mountaintop off the map.

Fat chance! Running down the ravine, he could see three more bugs taking cover. Their antennae were sticking slightly above the pile of boulders. These bugs must have spotted them after the grenades blew. They both dove behind the rocks on either side of the ravine trail. Matt had one rifle mortar left. He loaded it on the end of his rifle. Rob pulled the coordinates from his nocks and shouted them to Matt. Matt clicked on the setting. If this didn't work, they would be bottled, and the ravine's sides would be too steep to climb. Matt put the rifle butt on the ground and angled the barrel to the proper setting. He looked at the readout one last time. He said a little prayer as he pulled the trigger.

Kawoosh went the mortar. The explosive shell arched out of the ravine. Three long seconds later, it came down, and violent was an understatement for the explosion's sound. The three bug bodies, or at least many of their body parts, went flying. However, the explosion was much bigger than it should have been. When they reached the smoldering hole where the mortar had landed, they could see more body parts than could be explained by just three bugs. Gray metal pieces and the sickening smell of the bugs and explosives filled the air, and evidence of an ammo cache was strewn about, their luck was holding, and they quickly returned to running.

It would be three more miles to the extraction point, and they were still being pursued. They turned up the valves on their oxygen supplement bottles to compensate for the low oxygen content of the atmosphere. About halfway, Matt stopped long enough to set a grenade-sized mini-nuke charge and trip wires along the path. They had run another mile when the blast went off, but the wave of light had washed over them before they heard the nuke explode. Their suits, which were already protecting them from the background radiation, would protect them further from the mini-nuke, at least long enough to get off the planet. They could only hope that the blast took out the rest of their pursuers. They continued to run full tilt just the same.

Rob hollered that it couldn't be more than a few hundred yards until the surface opened into a small canyon. The dropship should be waiting. He'd call for them, but the bugs were superb at targeting radio transmissions. This whole affair had to stay radio silent. They came out of the ravine and into the canyon.

Matt did not see the dropship and went straight for cover, signaling Rob to do the same. Crouched behind more rocks, he scanned the gray-green sky. Looking back down, he saw a small red light blinking about a hundred yards to his left in the open canyon weeds. Rob's eyes blinked as well, then rubbed them to be sure of what he was seeing. They both leveled their rifles and were about to empty their magazines of caseless twelve-millimeter spent plutonium-tipped rounds on the red blinking light and anything around it.

A lone pilot appeared to step out from behind nothing. He waved for them to come over. He looked genuine enough, but from where did he come? Rob and Matt moved out from behind their cover, rifles leveled at the pilot's head. When they got close enough, the pilot identified himself and told them to get in, Rob thought the pilot was nuts, but as he got closer, he could see the air near the pilot, shimmering. Closer yet, and he could see, just barely, the outline of a small dropship. He could see the flash from the valley, just the other side of the ridge from which they had come, and the mushroom cloud rising above it. They jumped in what they hoped was an opening in the side of the camouflaged ship.

Once in, he heard the pilot tell them to hold on, and the ship jumped straight up. Rob was facing down, and the nine G take-off smashed his nose into the flooring, quickly breaking it. Matt had landed face up and was in decent shape as the ship neared ten thousand feet and went horizontal. The lurch of the vessel left his stomach somewhere behind him. Matt took the detonator from Rob's pocket and pressed the button as the ship sped away. As anticipated, the blast leveled the mountain.

The pilot explained that the ship was the newest extraction ship in the fleet. Its chameleon functions were the finest ever developed and worked well even on a planet as crappy as this one. It had just come in and would guarantee their safe extraction. However, they could not be contacted about it due to the radio silence order. With blood running down his face, Rob gave an evil appearance to Matt, but they both smiled and gave each other a high-five.

The ship made a few more course corrections, and the pilot told them to be ready for vacuum. They had found the chairs and strapped in, and the ship went horizontal again as violently as it did when it took off from the canyon floor. They looked out the viewport at the shrinking brown planet. Matt's body ached from the g-forces, but he didn't complain. He knew the maddeningly violent vector changes were the only way to confound any bug tracking and weapon deployment.

Rob figured another twenty-four hours, and he could be in the ship's infirmary having his nose fixed, and a shot of morph would feel really good, too, to say nothing of a shower, food, and plenty of sleep. They had completed every one of the requirements of their mission and escaped with minor damage. It was a fun challenge coming back to ancient earth for the training exercise.

Inconditus Verbum
Chapter 1

(CONFUSED WORD)

It was serendipitous, to say the least, that Maepinos of the House of New Science stumbled across a wonderous discovery. He had found that by lowering the temperature of the liquid of life, it would become solid. The result he named "Aeyce." The next discovery was even more accidental and more wonderous. While conducting the same experiment, a beaker became entangled in the wiring and spun around in the chamber. In so doing, it solidified in such a way that a hoolis was formed 1.5 diameters in the center of the liquid.

Lastly, while examining the hoolis with a probe, the end of the probe fell off, went down the hoolis, and completely disappeared. Where it went was the triumph of the Kikurace people. The probe end had folded space. It took a hundred years before the Kikurace learned to control the event. This control of space was known as Ishooarde, as in 'Ishooarding space.'

Maepinos, at the age of two hundred years, was elevated to a deity. Any wonderful occasion from then on was first exclaimed by the salutation "Blessed be Maepinos."

Chapter 2

THE KIKURACE WERE BREATHERS of liquid. Their planet had no dry land. When on an expedition, their environmental suits kept them in their aquatic state, supplying the correct amount of gases to their liquid of life. The system allowed them to sukor the liquid, this being a term used to explain breathing, therefore absorbing into their bodies and thus were sustained. On several expeditions through the hoolis, they encountered courk, a gas they found deadly; fortunately, courk was a rare commodity in their part of the galaxy.

The Kikurace spent the next thousand years exploring different parts of their galaxy, winding up on thousands of planets with aeyce. They would drop out of the fold of space and climb out of a similar hoolis or crevasse in the aeyce of another world. Many of the planets they encountered were abundant with resources, and minerals of all kinds, in liquid, gaseous and solid forms. However, no indigenous life beyond the smallest of aquatic and land animals had ever been encountered.

Therefore, it came as quite a surprise upon folding space into the polar regions of this new planet to find sentient beings. They were bipedal and large, enormous. The planet was filled with courk. These natives obviously were immune to the poison gas; in fact, it was observed, from afar, that the beings here might even use the courk to sustain their life functions, sukoring the way the Kikurace sukored the liquid of life. Moreover, these beings seemed very intelligent, they could be seen communicating with each other, and the Kikurace became excited about the idea of exchanging greetings as well as information on technology and medical advancements.

Chapter 3

THE KIKURACE HAD FOR years carried with them a translating device in hopes of meeting a race of people with whom they could communicate. It had worked well in their world to decode the many languages that were spoken. However, they had never before been able to test the device outside their own world because they had never found any other intelligent life.

John Hayes, a private first class in the United States Army, was standing watch in the guard shack of Post 29. It was the summer of 1955. Summer in Antarctica was still as cold as hell, but today it was sunny. John squinted out the window of the guard shack. Three small figures were headed his way. At first, he thought they were penguins. But, as the little squad of Kikurace got closer, the terror began to well up inside him. As they drew even closer, he could easily see these were far from penguins. He pulled his rifle off his shoulder and stepped out the door of the guard shack. They certainly weren't penguins, and as the figures came closer, the twitchier John's hands became. The visitors were wearing their normal environmental garb. Unfortunately, the suits they wore included bubble-type helmets, just like on the TV space monster shows. John aimed his rifle at the head of the first alien in line. With the shakiest squeakiest voice said.

"Stop...stop, where you are"!

The aliens stopped short, not because of the command John was shouting that they couldn't understand, but to look down at the translation device. The device needed to hear spoken language. It could then start to make calculations for interpretation. However, several problems began to arise. First, the words were being spoken in an oxygen gas, not through a liquid, and this caused the small machine a whole lot of problems.

John watched the aliens staring at a device. His knees were starting to weaken; he could only think about the movie in the barracks last night, "The Thing," starring James Arness as an alien bent of invading the Earth. He knew it was just a movie, but he also knew that this situation was not. He just wanted to get out of here. His bladder was ready to release. But he knew he couldn't put his weapon down.

"Who are you? What are you? What are you doing here? Where did you come from? You need to leave. No... wait... you need to stand still. I'll have to call this into the command center." He said shakily.

The aliens thought they had enough words for the processor. The first in line, the leader, looked at the screen of the translation machine. The translator explained that John wanted to know where they came from. The other two aliens hid directly behind the first; they had a little fear factor of their own, they were aware that some kind of weapon was being pointed at them. The leader looked up from the machine. He held out one hand holding a small box, pointed it toward the ground, and pressed the trigger. Next to the aliens, the ice started to melt. As it melted, it swirled like a flushed toilet. Then it froze, with a hole in the center. The alien was trying to show him what he thought John wanted to know.

John watched the ice melt and swirl and then freeze solid next to the aliens. He could also see the three-foot hole in the ice; by this time, he was shaking uncontrollably. Then, the alien, reading from the translator in his other hand and, with a face he thought would be pleasant, said to John,

"You courk sukors this are biggest aeyce hoolis. We Kikurace..."

The alien never got a chance to finish the what John thought was a threatening sentence. John pulled the trigger of his M1. A 30-caliber round went down the barrel and straight through the first alien's helmet and the helmets of the two aliens standing behind him. All three fell sideways into the hoolis. The hoolis melted, swirled, and was gone, leaving only flat ice.

The only thing the duty officer wanted to know was why Private Hayes had fired his rifle. The bullet was spent, and the empty shell casing was found in the snow. John spent hours, if not days, explaining what the aliens had said and how it sparked him to such violence. Unfortunately, the alien story was not well received by anyone, not the commander of the base, not the medical officer, and not the chaplain. The fact that no one would believe him drove John quite crazy, so much that his superiors had him confined to the infirmary. He eventually returned to the United States, where he was committed to a military hospital in Maryland.

Chapter 4

JOHN HAYES WAS RELEASED from The Walter Reed Health Care System Psychiatric Ward in 1975. After twenty years in the nut house, John found it curious that his story, for all its strangeness, wasn't even wanted by the obviously far-fetched tabloids. He died in 1995 at the age of 65, after a mediocre twenty-year career in Hollywood writing and directing sci-fi "B" movies. Even though some well-known actors and actresses had launched their career staring in John's movies, no one afforded him the respect to attend his funeral ceremony. He was buried in a pauper's grave site without a headstone.

The Kikurace discovered another three hundred planets in the following hundred years, and none ever had intelligent life. They never ventured to earth again, figuring there wasn't much intelligence there either and way too much courk.

Garbage In, Garbage Out Chapter 1

JAMAL NAJEET WAS JOYOUS. It was the first day of summer, June 21, and he had found a small hardware store selling the keychain laser pointers he had been looking for, for a mere dollar a piece. There were twenty left, and he bought them all. Two small aspirin-sized batteries powered each, and all the lasers were two inches in length. Jamal had an idea for a laser light projector but was hesitant to spend the money needed to purchase larger components that are more professional. Nevertheless, it was Friday evening, and he was happy that he had the whole weekend to work on his pet project.

His idea was to arrange the lasers in a circle. Each would point inward at a ten-degree tangent to the edge and be held in place by a small u-bolt. He had also glued twenty small, half-inch by half-inch mirrors on an inch-long threaded rod. The mirrors would be placed between each pointer to refine its direction further. These twenty pointers would do the trick. He had already built the round flange that would accommodate the pointers and mirrors, calculated the power requirements, and built the transformer he would need.

Jamal spent the evening drilling and soldering the parts together. Finally, close to midnight, the little project was finished. He set it on the workbench and turned it on. All the lasers fired, and there sat the most do nothing, unremarkable, unspectacular, lackluster, and mundane device he had ever constructed. The laser beams crossed and re-crossed each other creating what looked like a flat red lens, four inches in diameter. Jamal hoped the light show would have had a little more to offer. But, as it stands, it's not worth the electricity to turn it on.

As the night's last act, Jamal wrote down a few notes on what he might change to get a more exciting visual outcome. After a moment, he thought, "This sucks," and crumpled the notes into a ball. He tossed the paper ball toward the wastebasket at the other end of the workbench. The ball hit the adjacent wall and bounced directly into the center of the device. Jamal chuckled, "I couldn't make a shot like that if I wanted to," He said half-aloud.

Before turning the lights out for the night, he leaned over to get the ball of paper from under the device. Jamal liked to keep the workshop clean and tidy. The paper wasn't there. Jamal looked around and behind the device. The paper just wasn't there. For fear, his mind was playing tricks on him; he looked in the wastebasket. Nope, the paper ball was nowhere to be found.

Jamal leaned over the device and stared down through the glare of the rose-colored light. He could see the top of the wooden table below it. His hand reached over to the side, gathered another piece of paper, and balled it up. "If I recreate the situation, maybe it will show me where the ball deflected to," He whispered.

Jamal watched the paper ball drop into the device. He realized instantly that it did not fall through but completely disappeared as it passed through the plane of the light. Jamal backed up; his mouth hung open. He sat down on the workbench chair, his mouth still agape. He looked at the clock; it was after one in the morning.

"I'm tired, and this is just a hallucination brought on by sleep deprivation."

He turned the power off to the gadget, turned the workshop lights off, and went to bed.

Chapter 2

JAMAL SLEPT MOST OF the night fitfully. When deep comfortable sleep finally came, it was acutely interrupted by the beams of the summer morning golden sunlight in the blue sky, streaming through the window. Annoyed, he got up, still in his pajamas, and went straight to the coffee maker. He lived alone, and nobody was going to make it for him. While the coffee was brewing, he showered, shaved, and dressed. Then, with the fresh aroma of coffee wafting up his nose, he ventured to the workshop sipping his coffee along the way. He turned the machine on, balled up a piece of paper, and while again sipping his coffee, he let the ball drop onto the light. The ball disappeared as before, and his coffee cup hit the floor a moment later.

He decided now that the experience from the night before was not a dream or hallucination. But he still pinched his arm as a method to wake himself. He was now convinced that he was awake and proceeded to sweep and mop the coffee and broken cup. He returned to the kitchen, poured a new cup of coffee, and stood for a moment reflecting on what people said about people doing the same thing repeatedly, expecting a different result.

Back in the workshop, Jamal began experimenting with different materials. First, he dropped an orange pencil into the light. Typically, the pencil, being longer than the device is high, should have stopped with the eraser end sticking a few inches above the plane of the light. But no... it was gone. Likewise, nuts, bolts, a screwdriver, a fresh yellow banana, and the remainder of his morning coffee all disappeared into the rose-colored light.

Before this revelation of events, Jamal had wondered what would be the purpose of his ordinary-looking laser show device. Then, the light went off in Jamal's head. "I've been putting all my garbage in this thing," he exclaimed loudly to no one, for the workshop was empty.

He decided that the money he was worried about spending was no longer a concern and proceeded to build a new machine, only slightly bigger. After a frantic search, he found several more hardware stores selling larger and more powerful laser-pointing devices at a much higher price, but he didn't care.

Chapter 3

BY SATURDAY EVENING, Jamal finished the larger machine; it now projected a plane of laser light twelve inches in diameter. Everything was twice as big; there were forty laser pointers, forty deflection mirrors, and a larger transformer. Jamal did not cannibalize any of the parts from the original machine for fear the new device would not work. He turned the machine on and tossed a softball into it; sure enough, the softball disappeared.

It was now time for someone else to observe the machine. As strange as this might seem, Jamal was still apprehensive that what he was experiencing was not real. He invited a close friend over to the house to be a witness. Bob Young arrived at Jamal's home within a few hours.

"I would normally be spending Sunday morning with my wife and kids," said Bob, "But you seemed a little out of sorts Jamal," he continued. "Are you OK?" he finished.

" Yes, Bob, come in, come in, would you like some coffee?" Jamal said excitedly. Jamal could hardly contain himself. Bob took the coffee from his friend, and they entered the workshop.

"Well, it looks like you've been keeping yourself busy, Jamal," Bob said while looking at the machines and sipping the hot coffee.

"You'd better sit down, Bob," Jamal warned.

Jamal turned on the machine, and it silently started to produce the red plane of light inside the circle of laser pointers. Bob looked on and said it was "cute" but was unimpressed.

Jamal smiled. The next thing he did was to drop a grapefruit into the machine. The yellow citrus ball disappeared in front of Bob's eyes. Bob jumped up, spilling his coffee,

"That's quite a trick; how did you do that? I can't see any mirrors or lenses," Bob marveled.

"No trick, I swear, Bob. See for yourself," Jamal answered.

Bob examined the machine closely. He passed his hand over, under, and around the machine, finding nothing. He was about to pass his hand into the light when Jamal shouted, "Bob, don't do that. I'm not sure what would happen to your hand." Bob abruptly drew his hand back.

"That's totally awesome, Jamal; I have only one question, where did it go?" Bob queried.

Jamal had been so mystified by the disappearance of the items that the thought never occurred to him.

"I don't know, Bob," was his reply.

"Well, it has to go somewhere, doesn't it?" Bob asked.

Jamal had an idea. He had purchased a 'Car Key Tracker' because he was always misplacing his keys. If you press the little button on the tracker attached to the keys, it starts beeping. He retrieved it from another room. He dropped the tracker into the light. As usual, it, too, disappeared. Jamal pressed the button. He and Bob listened. There was no sound. They went to all the rooms in the house, pressing the button, but still nothing. They went all around the outside of the house, same results, zero sound.

The only reasonable explanation they could come up with is that the items placed in the light must have lost their molecular stability and dissolved, an excellent reason not to stick your hand in the light.

"Though you would think there would be some residual chemical occurrence, like when matter changes, you get heat," Jamal said.

Chapter 4

BOB HELPED JAMAL FIND every piece of garbage in the house that would fit in the hole. Organic and inorganic, it didn't matter; the more, the better. Next, Jamal went to the neighbor's houses and gathered their trash as well. Jamal and Bob proceeded to place everything in the hole. Within the hour, there was no trash left.

"Let me think aloud," Jamal said. "No fuming diesel bulldozers smashing down the trash, no hills or mounds, no smoke, no smell, minimal use of electricity. But, Bob, try to find a negative here," Jamal said fancifully.

"Sorry, Jamal, I can't at the moment find a reason not to become trash collectors.

We've worked at NASA long enough," Bob contemplated.

The next question was how big the machine can be and still function. So, Jamal Najeet and Bob Young agreed to build a much larger machine and begin collecting garbage. Startup costs would be minimal, with a truck or two, a large building to house the device, and some employees to toss in the trash.

"You know, Bob, up till now, we've only discussed domestic trash applications," Jamal said.

"Damn, you're right Jamal; I can think of a couple more just off the top of my head. How about waste oil or toxic chemicals that are currently injected underground? You know how the public hates that stuff." Bob quickly responded.

"Yes, but you missed a big one, Bob," Jamal said with a huge grin.

"What?" said Bob.

Jamal replied, still with the biggest ever grin, "Nuclear Waste, like spent fuel rods and such or even maybe warheads and Bio-weapons."

Chapter 5

JAMAAL NAZEETE HAD just sat down on the kitchen chair, sipping his coffae and watching the first of two blue-green suns rise in the yellow summer sky. It was the first day of summer, June 21. The smell of the morning meal his mate was cooking filled all four of his nostrils. He picked up his newspaper and began reading; a small ball of waded paper hit his head and fell to the floor. He looked down and saw more wadded paper. The kids must be up and playing. Within a moment or two, an orange pencil fell to the floor, followed by nuts, bolts, a screwdriver, and a yellow banana.

"What the hell is going on here?" he screamed as a warm brown liquid fell on his head.

WOW! Chapter 1

Marle Boro, an evening shift technician, had made a critical error but saved himself the embarrassment of letting the signal completely escape. The signal containment limits were clearly marked in red; on either side of the red mark were caution zones marked in yellow. It was technician Marle's responsibility not to allow any planetary signals to be broadcast toward a particular area of space. The equipment was automatic for the most part, but as old components were prone to breakdown, a technician was always on hand to manually adjust the machine if needed. Marle knew that an excursion into the yellow zone was not a high crime, but it showed a lack of responsiveness at his station and would be recorded on his logs. And forever be on his permanent record. He was mortified. He had trained for the last twenty years for this position and was hoping to move up the ladder and gain an even more prestigious position and relished the idea that the job would be on daytime duty.

He sat for the next hour, more concerned about the excuse he would give his superiors than his attention to the indicator board in front of him. The directional meter moved back and forth; while he stared at the view plate above, he continued to mumble different excuses he could use. His mind was clearly not on his responsibilities. The guidance needle burped and swung quickly into the red, alarms sounded, and the log printer began to buzz. Marle glanced down at the meter of the station controls, horrified. He fought with the controls for less than a minute until he brought the dial back to the safe area. It had only been in the red for a short period, seconds really; perhaps this would be a redeeming virtue. No one in the last hundred years, since the first contact and the beginning of the containment project, had allowed this to happen.

Over the years, as the reciprocity of the aliens increased and the population enjoyed the technological and medical advancements bestowed on them, the punishment for any aberrant radio transmission transgressions had gone from a simple reprimand to an ultimate capital criminal offense of treason. In the passing of these short seconds, he was ruined his career, his family, and his life.

Chapter 2

At the emergency meeting, the chief counsel, Abqua Bei, spoke first, "You are all aware of the containment transgression that occurred this morning. The question of punishment lies before us. Was the escape of the signal a fatal error? This will not be known during our lifetime. Therefore, the final sentence will not be made to technician Merle, but his descendants will suffer the punishment, as will all our grandchildren, should the signal be picked up and followed back to our world.

Nar Quandra was new to the council. He was aware of the containment requirements and the penalties for failure to obey the rules. But Nar, as well as many others new to the council, were not completely aware of why the rules existed or the reason for their extreme penalties. The rules were always the rules, but what was the cause, and from where did this particular rule come? He posed this question to Abqua Bei. "This project and its discipline are steeped in antiquity, and before we can provide judgment against the technician, please advise us what the containment is and why it should be of such importance," Nar said.

The frown on Abqua's face showed her feelings. Only an insolent young council member would question what the elders had held in high faith for a millennium. Abqua realized that this might be a delicate political moment. Time had reduced the number of elders on the council, and she had enjoyed her position as a committee leader for many years and wished it to remain so. She replaced her frown with a demure smile.

"A fair question Nar," she said.

"During the time of the First Contact, long before our industrial age began, but at the beginning of our communication era, we were offered admittance to the Galactic Union. The aliens told us they had watched us for a thousand years and found that we were beginning to acquire more advanced technology. They decided to make contact, and we were told of the many civilizations that existed in the universe. They said we would be helped by them and others and would be welcomed into the Union. We would and have received many advancements in the areas of energy, agriculture, resource management, and medicine. Our world is bountiful and peaceful. We were required to do only one thing in exchange for these blessings. It was the same thing that all members of the union did on each of their planets. We would be given equipment that would control when and where any radio signal would be sent, and this would allow the Union collective to remain hidden from beings known to be a vile race that might be searching for other life in the universe. Only one such race had been known to exist by the Union, and with the use of certain Union equipment, the Union and its members would always remain hidden."

"That's an acceptable answer," the young council member replied. "But, tell us, on what grounds do the aliens decide who is vile and who is acceptable to the Union?"

Abqua's face grew stern again, but she kept her composure with the young one.

"A race is vile if it wages war!" she retorted.

With that answer, the young council members' face flushed. Never had he been aware that any being would wage war with another. He thought 'war' was only a thing that happened in fantasy stories that were told as fables to the young so they would understand the horrors that must never be allowed to happen. It was part of the training one would go through to become an adult citizen. All the alien Union members were of the same upbringing. He returned to his seat, head down in embarrassment and contemplating what he had just heard, and fear that a warring race actually existed ran through his mind.

Abqua finished by explaining that the Union founders long ago began to study alien races and watched for the signs of intelligence to grow on each planet. If the growth evolved to a peaceful existence, then, at the correct time, First Contact would be made. If evolution went wrong, the planet would be put in quarantine. Eventually, the warring world would destroy itself long before it developed any space flight technology or at least traveled beyond its own solar system.

The council returned to the problem of the technician. The lost signal would take a hundred years to reach the quarantine area and another hundred years to know if the signal was detected. There would be a passing of several generations before they would know how much, if any, damage was done.

Chapter 3

Marle's felt his fate was sealed, and he did not take the humiliation well. He stood on the veranda of his dwelling, high on a mountainside, looking down over the capital city of Meesh. The great hall rose from the center. A white marble spire reaching to the sky, where the council met on matters of state. He knew they were meeting at this moment to decide his sentence. There had been no trial; the offense was too obvious and without any possible defense. Marle knew what the outcome would be and had mentally prepared himself.

Marle sat down at a table and slowly poured a drink. He added the poison carefully to the goblet. He drank from the glass ceremoniously while seated and died moments later.

The Boro family was now ostracized for the next two hundred years. Replacement technicians were trained more vigorously and supervised more intently. What Marle had done and the subsequent punishment stayed in the public conscience. The residents of the planet awaited their true fate for the next two centuries.

Chapter 4

On August 1977, the Ohio State "Big Ear" radio telescope received a signal. Sixty Janskys in a 10 kHz channel. When the tech on duty saw it, he could only exclaim, "Wow!" and wrote that word in the white space on the left side of the printout. The signal was fifty thousand times more potent than would ever have been expected and stood out on the page like a beacon. But search as they might, the technicians could not find a repeating occurrence.

Robert Graystone, an independent researcher, has been examining the signal for forty years. To date, the signal has never repeated itself, and Mr. Graystone has quantified it as a fluke not worth exploring. He has written various papers about how this signal appeared and how it would be without merit to spend resources to follow up on the signal's possible source.

A coded hyperspace signal is sent periodically, relaying a message to the Union: 'signal continues to be considered a fluke of nature, no action to trace the signal is expected. Will continue to follow and report on the activity of this culture...R.G. out.'

CARNIVORES
Chapter 1

IN A VERY STEALTHY manner, the invading forces had moved into position satellites with high-powered Electromagnetic Pulse generators (EMP). The satellites moved to coordinates that would place them equal distances apart, covering every square mile of the planet.

All major strategic weapon systems were rendered unusable during the first 24 hours of the Blaath invasion. The intensity of the EMP was shattering for the major powers across the globe. This included all aircraft, sea vessels, heavy armor, guns, tanks, and missiles, which each military authority thought had been hardened enough to sustain any such attack. What remained were elite ground forces from each country, with small and medium armament. These forces fought courageously and aggressively throughout cities and towns worldwide but to no avail. The Blaath invasion was relentless, vicious, and overwhelming in sheer number and technology.

Chapter 2

NODE 62, RECORDING Tron 80

Personnel Battle Log: Commander Taag Mocklik, Warrior, A-line penetration,

Subjugation Group, Blaath Battle Drop Vessel 26462.

Current Alien year 2052

This was the second day of the invasion of this planet. It is almost over, and the defending caste has all but been defeated. However, I have gained new knowledge, and it came as quite a surprise during a violent engagement with several inhabitants of this alien world. The combatants were from an elite military band named after a small furry water mammal. They were garbed in drab-colored clothing and wielding formidable weapons of different sizes. These warriors were also clad in what they considered weapon-resistant padding, which covered most of their vital organs.

I had to laugh because my molecular-edged battle sword always sliced neatly and without resistance through this padding. I had just dispatched three of the defenders with the sword held in my right hand. First, an upward swing disemboweling the oncoming enemy, then a downward swing beheading the second, and then a sideway slice cutting the last of the three in half, all while putting plasma rounds from the energy pistol in my left hand into the chest of two others all this while the last warrior leaped onto my chest, wielding an iron blade. The blade would not penetrate my chest plate even though the inhabitant tried vigorously and repeatedly to do so. With my hands full, my reaction was to throat bite the opponent and cause it to lose the ability to breathe.

I did so and was immediately surprised at the outcome. I ripped the neck ferociously, tearing out his windpipe and veins supplying blood to his brain. The warrior fell away, quivering with silent screams. I was finished with the battle, for no other living earthers remained around me, warrior or otherwise. It was then, during my battle reverie, that I realized how good this alien flesh tasted.

With all the assailants on the floor, either dead or dying, I had a few moments to chew and savor the meat freshly torn from the alien body. The flavor was delicious, better than I had ever tasted before. Normally during an invasion, when fighting with such intensity, there is, on occasion, a reason to use one's teeth, but until now, the flesh of other aliens was putrid and disgusting and only got by in the heat of battle.

I wondered if others in my group had the occasion to tear the flesh of the aliens in such a manner. Regardless, I pressed on, searching for other defending units to which I could slay or render helpless. These skirmishes would be over shortly, for the defenders were poorly equipped or trained to defend against our superior fighting skills, technology, and numbers.

I reported this occurrence immediately upon my return to the command center.

End of Log

Chapter 3

THE BLAATH FLAGSHIP landed heavily on the alien soil. As large as the ship was, the ground supported the ship's weight without consequence. Except that the ship's captain was executed for the rough landing that caused certain high officials some discomfort.

One of those officials, The Supreme Lord of Subjugation, sat at the Table of Decisions and, after reading the report of one of his invasion warriors, was enjoying a piece of human meat. His prehensile tongue plucked a small piece of meat stuck between his teeth. He did not bother to examine it further, and the fragment was taken down his gullet without further adieu. He continued to eat heartily from the leg bone of the defeated enemy.

After a hearty belch, he remarked aloud, "I may never leave this planet, for to space freeze this delicacy would be to diminish its flavor. Even thawed after freezing, it should still taste far better than any other meat currently sold in the galactic market," He finished.

His side mandibles angled up as he happily thought of the enormous amount of credits he would receive while in charge of this planet. The Consortium of Everlasting Flavor would become the most profitable food distribution enterprise ever to exist, and he would be given credit for its elevation.

The Blaath's usual mode of operation was to find, invade, conquer, subjugate the population, and extract the planet's resources. The population was enslaved for the purpose of labor. Many businesses governed the invasion policies of the Blaath. Earth, however, became an exciting change from the usual policy. The alien meat distribution of the animals found on different planets was always a big business but sentient beings, for the most part, were better at forced labor than they were for food.

Chapter 4

ON THE THIRD DAY, ORDERS came down from the High Command of the Subjugation Battle Group. All warriors are to refrain from damaging the planet's inhabitants unless absolutely necessary. Non-combatants must be treated well and not bruised. Food and water, and shelter should be readily available at all times.

The warriors grumbled as they rounded up the non-combatant Earthers. But complain as they may, no harm came to the prisoners; even the most hardened warrior knew the consequences of disobedience to the High Command would result in immediate execution.

Cages were built to accommodate the human population, and then as the numbers grew, concentration camps were established. These camps contained housing to keep the population warm and dry and cafeterias to feed the ever-growing numbers. Eventually, the camps became enormous, encompassing hundreds of acres of land. This necessitated shipping in water supplies and shipping out waste products.

The task initially seemed impossible, but with the resources and experience of the Blaath invasion force, the task was soon completed, and humans were gathered by the thousands and tens of thousands into the many Blaath internment camps.

Many escape attempts were tried but to no avail. The humans involved in the attempts found themselves at the front of the processing line.

Chapter 5

SEVERAL NERVOUS UNDERLINGS were seated at the Table of Decisions. The Supreme Lord had just finished eating a piece of human and demanded to know why it did not have the delicious flavor of previous human meals.

One of the underlings by the name of Namby Washup sheepishly stood, bowed, and asked if he could speak. The Supreme Lord gave permission but with the understanding that he would execute the underling himself unless he got a reasonable answer. With his knarled hand gripping the hilt of his bejeweled sword, he said: "Speak."

The underling, having gathered much information on where the meat had come from, quickly explained that the human in question was much older than the others he had eaten. In fact, the alien had volunteered to be the meal so that others would not be consumed. The alien had been nearly ninety of this planet's years of age. The underling had surmised that with this age, the meat had become sinewy and may have less flavor.

The Supreme Lord eyed the underling menacingly. "What should we do with the old ones?"

The underling, an astute student of both politics, culinary arts, and court protocol, explained that the old ones could be boiled and simmered down, rendering a condensed flavor and used in making a most delicious soup; thus, not wasting any of the population and contributing to the Consortium profit coffers.

The Supreme Lord's mandibles turned at such an angle of happiness that they almost broke. Then, with his jeweled sword flying expertly through the air, the Supreme Lord himself summarily executed all the underlings. Except for Washup, standing in his own urine, who he elevated, as was his supreme right, to an executive position in charge of commodity research.

Chapter 6

CHIEF EXECUTIVE WASHUP, guarded by a squad of warriors, was investigating a grocery store in a small town near his research facility. The local inhabitants had previously ransacked the store during the first weeks of the invasion. Washup felt he had to know precisely what the alien diet included to keep the humans healthy and well-fed.

Unfortunately, the store was so empty that it offered little help understanding human dietary standards. However, in a corner, he saw a pile of debris and in it found a rectangularly shaped can that had been kicked to the side. He began examining the ingredient label; by this time, he had picked up much human language regarding their food and was able to decipher the label. A bright light went off in his red fluffy feathered head.

Exotic animal meat from other captured planets was usually processed, cut, flash-frozen, and shipped to hundreds of Blaath-conquered worlds and colonies across the galaxy. It was a logistical nightmare to ensure adequate distribution of nutritional needs on a galactic scale. Many civilizations, overcome by the Blaath, were rich in minerals but short on agriculture and population. Therefore, it became imperative to feed both the Blaath and the native slave populations to continue to extract the local resources of those planets. Even in the deep space freeze, the meat would lose some quality.

Now, however, came Namby's novel idea, he could prepare the flesh, add spices and preservatives, use all of the previously undesirable parts, including the entrails, brain, eyes, and ground bone, and pack it in a can. The can even came with its own opening device, much the same as the can he had picked up in the grocery store.

Of the original eight billion humans, five billion remained after the invasion. This would be a spectacular sustainable natural resource if kept in reasonable condition.

The Consortium of Everlasting Flavor readily accepted this idea to limit waste and increase profits. Of course, it did not suit everyone's appetite, but it was accepted by the Supreme Lord and so many others that Namby was again elevated in stature. The now Senior Chief Washup flushed with pride even deeper than his already red-feathered body.

Chapter 7

SENIOR CHIEF WASHUP dabbled in his laboratory, happily experimenting with different food preparation methods. As he found a particular recipe he liked, he would try it out on one of the dozen warriors assigned to the security of his research facility. The warriors were always ravenous and never turned down a chance to eat.

However, on rare occasions, a platter to be tested was not quite as tasty as Washup thought, and the warrior's battle sword was halfway out of its sheath before the warrior realized with whom he was dealing. A Blaath elevated as many times as Namby was to be obeyed the same as a Lord;

Washup handed the food to the warrior and backed away quickly. It bordered on dangerous, but the warrior caste was the largest population in Blaath society. If a warrior liked the food, then everyone liked the food.

Washup added to the recipe certain specific ingredients, cooked and stirred the pot. He dipped his foreclaw in the pot and tasted the result. His eyes sparkled. Washup embarrassingly started to drool.

"This must be the best recipe I have concocted since; I don't know, *ever!*" He shouted.

A warrior stationed a few yards away rolled his eyes in disdain, thinking he would be chosen as taster today. But, as the wonderful aroma drifted past him, he, too, started to drool.

A particular spice used by the Blaath and the other carnivore races throughout the galaxy was hitherto unknown to the people of Earth. The spice came from a planet far at the end of another arm of the galaxy and was used extensively by everyone. The Alcospice, however, did a strange thing but only when added to human meat. It caused an infinitesimal amount of Spicazine to be produced. Spicazine, in large quantities, is lethal to most non-human species and is always accumulative in the aliens.

Needless to say, human meat, spice, and all were delivered to the entire galaxy in very, very large numbers.

Chapter 8

THE NEXT TWENTY EARTH years devastated the Earth's population as the earthlings were harvested, but it was even worse for non-humans. The meat, eaten haughtily, had slowly but thoroughly and, most important, unknowingly poisoned everyone in the Blaath sphere of influence, and the worst poisoning came from the flesh processed in cans, which was inexpensive to process and purchase because the seasoning was the most popular. As a side effect, the poisoning caused muscle loss and infertility, and the Blaath populations became sterile, and their numbers diminished rapidly.

The Blaath, as a race, were rendered deathly ill, from the highest elevated Lord to the lowest sub-warrior and weapons cleaner. The warrior caste became too weak to constrain the human population. Humans, on the other hand, had been kept fed and healthy for processing during the entire time of subjugation. They were given food grown in their own fields or beef raised in the camps. They were never fed the meat of their own species. The Blaath on Earth grew weaker and were ultimately deposed, and it was an ugly uprising. Slaughter took place around the world. What would you expect from a race that had been subject to worldwide cannibalism? No Blaath on Earth was left alive, regardless of gender or age. It seemed a fitting retribution under the circumstances.

Unknown to Earth, the remaining Blaath populations across the galaxy were nearly decimated by the poisoning and gave little concern to Earth and its humans during their recovery.

A century passed, and Earth regained some of its population. Technology flourished with the help of Blaath machines and vessels taken during the revolution. Weapons research advanced rapidly because the fear of the Blaath returning was always on the minds of the humans.

No Blaath ever returned, and Earth, with its new weapons and ships, began its quest for the stars, one of the dreams taken during the invasion. One prime goal was at the forefront of Earth's desires. That goal was to remove Blaath's existence from the universe and any indication of the atrocities that Earth had endured.

Chapter 9

BEFORE THE BATTLEFLEET left Earth, a conference of nations had been held. The question for discussion was how Earth would deal with the Blaath civilization. The ethics of genocide was on the table for discussion. Destroy them all, or conquer? There are doves and hawks, and there are those vengeful and those forgiving.

A representative from each Earth nation came to the podium and began reciting the names of those who had died since the invasion. Three billion were killed in the war. Five billion more were eaten over the next twenty years. There was no nation that had not suffered the torment of seeing friends and relatives taken to the slaughterhouses. All humanity was involved; no race was spared. There was no one who would claim that the atrocity never happened. Twenty-four hours a day, the names were spoken, and after thirty days, the readings were called to a halt. Any dissenters still wanting to show mercy on the Blaath left the conference after a few days.

The first Earth fleet ever to enter the Blaath Empire entered orbit around the Blaath homeworld. High-resolution cameras aboard the flagship 'Nuremberg' showed the world in complete disrepair. The camera also picked up a huge sign on the side of what looked like a distribution center. The AI on board interpreted the sign and put the caption at the bottom of the screen. The caption sent a collective gasp across the entire fleet.

It read, "Over 60,000,000,000,000 Sold".

"All ships, prepare to destroy the planet, on my command," Admiral Weinkoff calmly spoke into the microphone. "Commence bombardment" were his next words, spoken with the hate of generations lost.

Forty minutes later, he spoke again. "Ceasefire." There was only rubble left of the Blaath homeworld.

The fleet left in search of any Blaath colonies they could find with the intent of total destruction. On several occasions, a Blaath settlement was found, and the few remaining inhabitants begged for mercy. None was given.

Many years have passed, and it is believed that all of the Blaath are

dead, but the search continues just the same.

Commercial Traveler
Chapter 1

LOOKING OUT THE WINDOW, I watch a small bird eyeing the solitary shrunken fruit hanging lonely, abandoned by the leaves of autumn, on the naked twig. Startled, as we started up, the bird snatches the small blackberry from the bush and flies away. It was only a 25-mile trip to the Airlines Parking lot. "Follow the shuttle bus," I am told, to the appropriate parking area. Park. Get on the shuttle and ride to the airport, another few miles. So, I did.

The shuttle pulls up to the terminal, and I depart, thinking how much I hate going out of town. I should have been a writer; then, I wouldn't have to work so hard for a living. Oh well, another day, another dollar. Going into the terminal now, isn't that a horrible name for an airport building? I look for the appropriate line to enter to get through the security check.

I read the signs that tell me what not to bring on board the plane matches or lighters are on the list, as well as any liquid more than an ounce. I must ensure all the right things are put in the baskets, watch, cell phone, pocket change, and comb. Oh yeah, belt, shoes, jacket, and, of course, my carry-on bag. God forbid I would be the guy who's holding up the line. I wait patiently and am called to the magnetometer. I walk through and hear no beeps or bloops. Thinking I was all but done, another security guard called me to a second area.

A new machine! The guard beckons me to go in; standing there, I'm told to stand on the yellow feet painted on the floor, hands out to my sides, palms down. The machine swirls around me. Next, he says to turn and stand on the green feet, I turn 90 degrees, and this time hands extended out in front, again, palms down. The machine swirls again. Then the guard says,

"Okay, come over here and have a seat."

He points to a simple plastic chair. I sit and watch suspiciously as he puts on the blue latex gloves. He says to me,

"I'll have to check the bottoms of your feet."

I looked at him with a grin and said, "Whatever you say, Doc." He laughs.

After checking my feet for God knows what, he calls on his radio to get a final clearance. Who he called and where they might be is a mystery. The clearance comes, and I'm on my way to get dressed again. Well, I sure feel safe, if nothing else. Putting everything back on and grabbing my carry-on luggage, I head for the Sky Bar lounge.

Chapter 2

THE SKY BAR LOUNGE is noisy, but it's the only place for a smoke in the terminal. If I look up, there are 15 different flat panels to see, none of which is playing anything I want to watch. I'm not a sports fan.

I find an empty table and sit patiently. I'm way ahead of schedule. Fear of getting here too late forces me to get here too early. I've got enough to read, but as usual, I'll most likely be asleep before we even take off; planes really bore me. I guess I'm lucky. I've been on little planes, and the wakeful tension is from watching the pilot who couldn't be out of high school yet climb into the pilot seat. Now, that keeps me awake.

I order a Diet Coke and look around the bar. A hundred faces, those not talking to traveling companions, sit contemplating, sipping on coffee. Others are looking around or at the screens of the flat panels. Some are on cell phones smiling, some with pursed lips, and some in a heated discussion. Finally, some walked out with their wheeled American Tourister suitcases in anticipation of a droll travel day just like me.

I see Detroit's Fox 2's news anchor Cam Carmon on the TV screen. I can read the larger headline at the bottom of the screen, but there's heavy music playing, conversation all around, and her words elude me. It's closing in on nine o'clock, so I gather my things and look for the waitress to get me a bill for my Coke. I smoke my last Marlboro that I lit with matches I got from the waitress, which I will put in my pocket. So why did I have to give them up in the security line? Who knows.

The walk is easy. Moving runways take me most of the way. It gives me time to see more faces and contemplate where these people might be going. Some, dressed for hot weather, are a dead giveaway in the crisp early spring of Michigan. I wish plaintively I was on vacation, but still, I'm headed for Georgia's Atlanta Hartsfield Airport; maybe the weather there will give me a break.

The Otis motorized walkway ride is leisurely. It gives me time to observe storefronts, men, kids but mostly the women. As I move on the walk, they come toward me, pass, and then move away. Moving toward me, I can judge them by their cleavage, firmness, or perkiness. And while moving away, I can score them for their derriere—sixes and sevens, for the most part, an occasional eight, and very few nines. There were no tens anywhere in sight; well, some have it, and some don't. What a chauvinist I am. But the ride is long, and the temptation is great. Maybe that's God's conspiracy because no matter where I'm headed, my boarding area is always at the far end of the terminal.

Halfway down the terminal, you're forced to get off the walkway almost in front of the Borders bookstore. Should I go in? Why not! I enter, not looking for anything, just looking, and not sure if I like to read more or write more. Having thought that I have played every Halo game and read every Halo book, I spot a new title, "The Cole Protocol" this is fantastic; what a find. Yup, I'm sure there is a guiding hand involved. "*Go into the store, you'll be happy, go into the store,*" was the chant by the evil spirit of unlikely chance. Purchasing the book, I exited the store and continued down to the end of the terminal to find the boarding area.

Over an hour to go before boarding the plane, I sit, and the overwhelming boredom begins to set in. I'll try to read, but I'm sure my eyes will be closing soon. I sit with a book in one hand and tightly grasp my luggage with the other, airport security, you know. Keep your carry-on luggage secure. I begin to read my new book. As I had hoped, the book begins immediately with battles between aliens and humans. These books start with battles and usually stay that way throughout the book.

"Will first-class ticket holders and those needing special assistance please begin boarding," rings out over the load speaker.

Chapter 3

FIRST-CLASS TICKET holders virtually run to get ahead of any wheelchairs that might get in the way. Finally, my turn comes to get on the plane; as it turns out, my seat is the window seat on the plane's last row. Seated and buckled, I begin waiting and waiting. I usually try to keep clothes and toiletries to a minimum, so if I can cram everything just right, it all goes in a bag that slides easily under the seat in front of me. Everyone else is searching for space in the overhead compartment. There is never enough room because some idiots have carry-on luggage the size of a footlocker. So, I will wait some more.

I always get the window seat that way; my rolled-up jacket, acting as a pillow, is laid against the bulkhead, my hat gets pulled down over my eyes, and bingo, I'm drowsing out. I can barely feel the acceleration, then the lift-off, and then a gentle turn. I peek out under the bill of my hat and see the clouds as the wing cuts through them. Past the clouds, the bright sun breaks through, and I pull the bill of my cap down over my eyes.

Chapter 4

I SUPPOSE SOME TIME went by, and I felt the heavy slam from below and then the screams. Startled, I looked out the window. Below the plane, I see a large flat metal object, much bigger than the plane, so big in fact, the edge of the disk stretched farther away than the wings and obliterated the view of the ground below. The object had slammed the plane from beneath. It had felt like a hard landing.

Ahead and to the right, the floor erupted. Shards of metal were thrown everywhere. Smoke and flame flew up from the eruption. From the resultant opening, an alien warrior appeared in the hole and climbed up into the cabin. Clad in dark-colored armor with gold trim, his appearance was immediately menacing. The alien's clawed feet grabbed at the dark blue floor carpeting. His face was mostly a viciously sharp beak, like that of an eagle or hawk, smaller dark eyes and adorned with a tight royal blue helmet. His three-hinged legs, although bi-pedal, made him look awkward. Weapons in both his hands began firing as he moved forward. A second warrior jumped out of the hole. The two of them easily and quickly killed humans on their way toward the first-class section.

The first-class passengers scream no differently than coach. There was no place to run; there was no place to hide the aliens killed all but one of the passengers in the front of the plane. The remaining well-dressed gray-haired man leaned away in horror. One of the warriors grabbed him by the neck and pulled him up from the seat. Holding his neck, enough to be uncomfortable, but still allowing him to breathe. The other alien fired his weapon continually through the bulkhead door that separated the captain and crew from the rest of the plane. In moments the door melted into nothingness. Burning, charred bodies were all that remained of the flight crew. The two aliens now dragged the white-haired man back to the hole from which they had entered. The white-haired man gasping for air, made a few gurgled comments before they threw him in the hole.

"I'm a senator..." "You can't..." "Please, let's make a deal..."

And just before entering the hole, his last words were

"Damn commercial airlines."

The alien turned and fired the plasma weapon at the person occupying the aisle seat in my row. The passenger slumped back into the seat with a burn hole through his head. Then, just as quickly, the alien weapon erupted again, killing the person immediately next to me. The alien weapon, now aimed at me, went off. My vision blurred. I thought it would be more painful.

The alien ship peeled over to the right, and the jet fell off. It would tumble the remaining five miles to the ground.

Something was bumping into my shoulder. It became annoying as I was trying to die peacefully. I felt more tapping.

"Sir, sir, please, please."

My vision started to clear; I focused on a gleaming gold Northwest Airlines nameplate engraved with the name Maggie. As my vision cleared, even more, I looked up to see the '10' I had not seen in the terminal. The flight attendant continued.

"Sir, please wake up; you need to de-plane now."

A shudder ran through me. Then, gaining reality, I felt my face to see if I had drooled. I tried to smile as I unbuckled my seatbelt, grabbed my bag, and juggled across the other two seats. Where the dead bodies used to be. I sheepishly made my way down the aisle toward the exit. I chuckled to myself as I walked down the aisle. I've got to stop falling asleep in public.

Don't miss out!

Visit the website below and you can sign up to receive emails whenever J.J. Smiley publishes a new book. There's no charge and no obligation.

https://books2read.com/r/B-A-NBSE-NPBY

BOOKS 2 READ

Connecting independent readers to independent writers.

Also by J.J. Smiley

All That Remains
Coven; Short Stories of Sci-fi and Fantasy
The Tree
Girls
Run!

About the Author

Disappointed with titles that I read or watched in the theatre, it was time to write my own adventures. Just writing for personal pleasure at first and then publishing, has now become a joyful pastime.

My wife who is always watching my back convinced me to go to press.

www.ingramcontent.com/pod-product-compliance
Lightning Source LLC
Chambersburg PA
CBHW031413160726
47993CB00003B/1220